THE SQUIRREL

THE CROW

THE OWL

THE 'POSSUM

THE RACCOON

ANIMAL BOOK

THE BEAR

THE WOODCHUC

THE TURTLE

THE CHIPMUNK

THE RABBIT

SQUIRREL

THE CROW

THE OWL

POSSUM

ANIMAL BOOK

THE BEAR

THE WOODCHUCK

HE RACCOON

E TURTLE

THE CHIPMUNK

THE RABBIT

OTHER BOOKS BY INEZ HOGAN

THE TWIN SERIES

Twin Colts
Monkey Twins
Twin Deer
Twin Seals
Mule Twins
Twin Lambs
Raccoon Twins

Kangaroo Twins
Twin Kids
Elephant Twins
Bear Twins
Giraffe Twins
Koala Bear Twins
Twin Kittens

Twin Puppies

THE NICODEMUS BOOKS

Nicodemus and the Goose
Nicodemus and the Gang
Nicodemus and the Houn'dog
Nicodemus and His Little Sister

Nicodemus and the Little Black Pig
Nicodemus and His New Shoes
Nicodemus Laughs
Nicodemus Runs Away

THE NAPPY BOOKS

Nappy Chooses a Pet
Nappy Planted a Garden
Nappy Wanted a Dog
Nappy Is a Cowboy
Nappy Has a New Friend

THE READ-TO-ME BOOKS

About Nono, the Baby Elephant
About the Littlest Cowboy
About Peter Platypus
About Charlie

BOOKS NOT IN SERIES

We Are a Family
World Round
A Party for Poodles
A Bear Is a Bear
The Upside Down Book
Me
The Little Ones
The Big Ones
The Littlest Satellite
The Littlest Bear
Monkey See, Monkey Do
Little Lost Bear
The Lone Wolf

CUBBY BEAR
AND THE BOOK

A READ WITH ME BOOK

STORY AND PICTURES BY

INEZ HOGAN

E. P. DUTTON AND COMPANY, INC.

THIS BOOK IS DEDICATED
TO YOU

Copyright, ©, 1961 by INEZ HOGAN
All rights reserved. Printed in the U.S.A.

FIRST EDITION

No part of this book may be reproduced in any form without
permission in writing from the publisher, except by a reviewer
who wishes to quote brief passages in connection with a review
written for inclusion in a magazine, newspaper or broadcast.

Published simultaneously in Canada by Clarke, Irwin & Co., Ltd. of Toronto

Library of Congress Catalog Card Number: 61-12448

FOREWORD

This is a book designed to interest the pre-school child in reading. In the first part of the book, which should be read to the child by an adult, a little girl leaves her book in the woods. Cubby Bear and his friends find the book. "What is this strange thing?" they ask. They learn that a book opens. When they see their own pictures on the pages, they become very interested. But what are the little rows of black things under the pictures? The crow even tries to eat them!

After the little girl returns to the woods and finds her book, she reads it to the animals. This second part of the story, a "little book within the book," has a controlled vocabulary of only twenty-one words repeated several times. It is to be read by the child.

But CUBBY BEAR AND THE BOOK is not a primer; rather, it introduces the child to reading. It is a *fun* book that will encourage children to want to read, and to enter the wonderful world of books.

INEZ HOGAN
New York

CUBBY BEAR AND THE BOOK

Once there was a little black bear cub named Cubby.

He lived in a hollow tree and he was always peeping out to see what went on in the big woods.

One day he saw a little girl sitting under his tree. She was reading a book.

Cubby had seen children in the woods before. They were always running and playing. But what was that little girl looking at?

Cubby Bear had never seen a book before.

So he climbed up in the tree to
get a better look at it.

A raccoon was peeping out of his
hole. "Look!" he said. "Look what's going
on down there under the tree."

Cubby looked down. He saw a boy
calling to the little girl. The little
girl jumped up and dropped
the book. Then she ran out of the
woods with the boy. She forgot her
book. There it was lying on the
ground under the tree.

"Look!" said Cubby. "She left that
thing down there."

"What is it?" asked the raccoon.

"I don't know," said Cubby Bear.

"What are you looking at?" said a 'possum who was hanging by his tail from a branch in the tree.

"We're looking at that thing down there under the tree. Do you know what it is?"

"No," said the 'possum, "but the woodchuck is coming out of his hole. He's look-ing at it too."

"Come on," said Cubby Bear. "Let's go down and get it before he does."

So the 'possum, the raccoon and Cubby climbed down out of the tree in a hurry.

Cubby Bear picked up the book.

"Look!" he cried, "a picture of me! It belongs to me. It's mine!"

"I saw it first," said the woodchuck.

"No you didn't," said the 'possum. "I was hanging in the tree and I saw it before you peeped out of your hole. It's mine."

"It belongs to Cubby Bear," said the raccoon.

"Well," said Cubby, "can any of you tell me what it is?"

"Maybe it's good to eat?" said the 'possum. "That's silly," said the raccoon.

"What is all this fuss about?" said a tiny chipmunk, crawling out of his hole in the ground.

"Come out and see," said Cubby.

He stood the book up against
the tree so the tiny chipmunk could
see. "Now, tell me," said Cubby Bear,
"what is that?"

"I don't know what it is," said the
chipmunk, "but I do know that it
does not belong to you or raccoon
or 'possum or woodchuck. It belongs
to a little girl. I was peeping out
of my hole. I saw her looking at it."

"Of course," said Cubby. "I saw her too,
but she ran off and left it here.
If she comes back to look for it
I'll give it to her. I don't even know
what it is."

"Well," said the chipmunk, "here comes
a rabbit. Maybe he knows."

So Cubby Bear called the rabbit. "None of us knows what this thing is," said Cubby.

The rabbit looked at the book standing there under the tree. "Did it grow up out of the ground?" he asked.

"No, it did not," said Cubby Bear.

"Did it fall down out of the tree?"

"No, it did not," said the tiny chipmunk.

"Can it walk and talk?" asked the rabbit.

"Of course not," said a turtle, sticking his head out of his shell.

"Then it's nothing," said the rabbit. "Nothing at all."

"It must be something," said the turtle.

"Caw! Caw!" said a crow flying down out of the tree. "You're right, turtle. It must be something because you can see it."

"Of course," said the turtle. "If it is nothing we could not see it."

"You're right," said the crow. "We *can* see it, but what is it? Everything has a name. I'm a crow. You're a turtle.

"I'll take a peck at it. I'll find out what it is."

"Stop pecking at that," said the turtle, the raccoon, the bear and the chipmunk, all at one time.

"I have to peck at it to be sure it is something," cawed the crow.

"Can't you see it?" asked the bear.

"Yes," said the crow. "I'm sure it is something, but I don't know what it is. I will ask the owl. He's a wise old fellow who lives in a hole up there in the tree."

"That's a good idea," said Cubby. "We'll all go with you."

So the crow flew up in the tree.

The animals climbed up, all except the
turtle and the rabbit. They couldn't climb.

The crow peeked in the hole where
the wise owl lived.

"Go away," screeched the owl. "I
sleep all day. Go away!"

"We just wanted to know what this
is," said Cubby Bear holding the
book up.

"I can't see in the daytime," said
the owl, sticking his head out of the
hole. "Go away."

"We'll *never* find out what this thing
is," said Cubby.

"I know what it is," said a squirrel, sticking his head out of a hole in the tree.

"Good," said Cubby. "Come on down out of the tree and tell us."

"We can't go down now," said the squirrel. "Look, the fox is down there."

"He's chasing the rabbit," said the 'possum.

"The fox won't catch him," said Cubby. "That rabbit can run fast."

"He won't catch the turtle. He can hide in his shell," said the squirrel.

"And he can't catch us," said the tiny chipmunk. "The fox can't climb a tree. He's gone now. Let's go down."

So they all sat down under the
tree and the squirrel began.

"I used to live in a park."

"What is a park?" asked the 'possum.

"A park," said the squirrel, "is a place
where children come to play.

"Some of them bring things like
this to the park. They sit down on the
grass and open them up like this."

"It opens!" shouted the animals.

"But you haven't told us what it is,"
said Cubby Bear.

"Look!" cried the crow. "The
little girl is coming. She's looking
under all the trees. She's looking for
that. Let me fly over with it so
she'll know that we found it."

"That's a good idea," said Cubby Bear.

Then the crow picked up the book in his claws and flew up in the air calling, "Caw! Caw! Here it is. Here it is."

The little girl saw the crow. She saw her book. "It's mine," she shouted. "That's my book."

"Caw! Caw!" cried the crow. "Follow me."

And the little girl followed the crow back to the tree where the animals were waiting.

"MY BOOK!" cried the little girl. "You found my book."

"A BOOK!" said Cubby. "Now we know what it is."

"A BOOK! A BOOK!" shouted the animals, all at one time.

"What do you do with it?" asked Cubby Bear.

"You read it," said the little girl, "and look at the pictures."

"We looked at the pictures," said Cubby, "but we *can't* read."

"Then I will read it to you," said the little girl. "I *can* read."

So they all sat down under the tree and the little girl opened the book.

"Look!" cried the crow, "a picture of ME! What are those little black things standing in a row under my picture? They look like little black bugs." He took a peck at them.

"Those little black things are not bugs," said the little girl. "They are letters. Letters standing in a row make words, and words say something."

"What do the words under my picture say?" asked the crow.

"They say 'The Crow,'" said the little girl. "Now I'll read the book to you."

TURN THE PAGE
AND READ THE BOOK.

THE CROW

The crow can fly.

THE RABBIT

The rabbit can run.

THE TURTLE

The turtle can crawl.

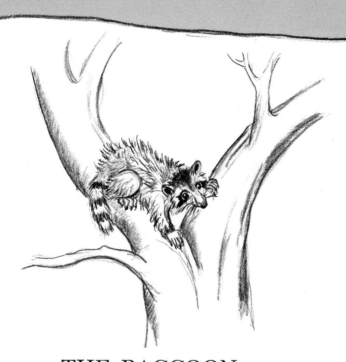

THE RACCOON

The raccoon can climb.

THE 'POSSUM

The 'possum can hang
in the tree.

THE SQUIRREL

The squirrel lives in a hole
in the tree.

THE WOODCHUCK

The woodchuck lives in a hole
in the ground.

THE CHIPMUNK

The chipmunk lives in a hole
in the ground.

"And I live in a hole in this tree,"
screeched the owl.

"It must be getting late," said the littl
girl. "The owl is awake.

"I must go home. I live in a house."

GOOD BYE!" shouted all the animals.
Come back soon."

'I'll come back," said the little girl. "And

'll bring another book to read to you.

READING IS FUN."

THE SQUIRREL

THE CROW

THE OWL

THE 'POSSUM

ANIMAL BOOK

THE BEAR

THE WOODCHUCK

THE RACCOON

THE TURTLE

THE CHIPMUNK

THE RABBIT

SQUIRREL

THE CROW

THE OWL

POSSUM

ANIMAL BOOK

THE BEAR

THE WOODCHUCK

THE RACCOON

E TURTLE

THE CHIPMUNK

THE RABBIT